Books by Margaret J. Anderson

FICTION
To Nowhere and Back, 1975
In the Keep of Time, 1977
Searching for Shona, 1978
In the Circle of Time, 1979
The Journey of the Shadow Bairns, 1980
Light in the Mountain, 1982
The Brain on Quartz Mountain, 1982
The Mists of Time, 1984
The Druid's Gift, 1989
The Ghost Inside the Monitor, 1990

NONFICTION
Charles Darwin, Naturalist, 1994
Bizarre Insects, 1996
Isaac Newton, 1996
Carl Linnaeus, Prince of Botany, 1997
Children of Summer: Henri Fabre's Insects, 1997

CHILDREN OF SUMMER

Children of Summer

HENRI FABRE'S INSECTS

Margaret J. Anderson

Pictures by Marie Le Glatin Keis

Frances Foster Books · Farrar, Straus and Giroux · New York

In memory of Annegret Dieterich
1984–1996
—MARGARET J. ANDERSON

To Joa and Quena
—MARIE LE GLATIN KEIS

Text copyright © 1997 by Margaret J. Anderson
Pictures copyright © 1997 by Marie Le Glatin Keis
All rights reserved
Published simultaneously in Canada by HarperCollinsCanadaLtd
Printed in the United States of America
Designed by Lilian Rosenstreich
First edition, 1997

Library of Congress Cataloging-in-Publication Data
Anderson, Margaret Jean.
    Children of summer / Margaret J. Anderson ; pictures by Marie
Le Glatin Keis—1st ed.
        p.   cm.
    "Frances Foster books."
    Summary: Ten-year-old Paul describes how he and his sisters
learned about insects from the observations and writings of their
father, the nineteenth-century French entomologist Jean-Henri Fabre.
    ISBN 0-374-31243-5
    1. Fabre, Jean-Henri, 1823–1915—Juvenile fiction. [1. Fabre,
Jean-Henri, 1823–1915—Fiction. 2. Entomologists—Fiction.
3. Insects—Fiction. 4. France—Fiction.] I. Le Glatin Keis, Marie,
ill. II. Title.
PZ7.A54397Ch   1997
[Fic]—dc20   96-16937

Author's Note

Jean Henri Fabre (1823–1915) was a famous explorer, yet he seldom left his own backyard. He spent his whole life discovering the secrets of the insect world. Fabre had a brilliant mind, but what made him a great scientist was his never-ending curiosity and patience. His home and its surroundings served as his laboratory. His lab assistants were his wife and children. The entire family shared his passion for insects, especially his youngest son, Paul.

In his final book, Fabre wrote: "From time to time, a few truths are revealed, tiny pieces of the vast mosaic of things . . . Others will come who, also gathering a few fragments, will assemble the whole into a picture ever growing larger but ever notched by the unknown."

—M.J.A.

Contents

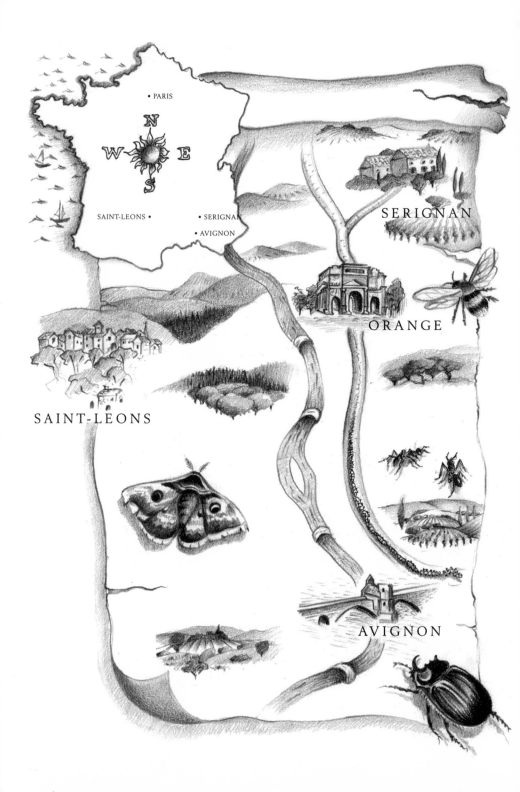

CHILDREN OF SUMMER

The Hermit of Sérignan

My father's name is Jean Henri Fabre. His friends call him Henri, but I call him Père, and the people around here call him the Hermit of Séri-gnan because he rarely goes into the village. A hermit is someone who lives in solitude, but Père does not live alone. He has his family for company. There's my mother, Marie, and my sisters, Anna and Marie-Pauline. Anna is five and Marie-Pauline is eight. And, of course, there's me—Paul. I am ten. Père also has his "children of summer." That's what he calls the insects that visit the wildflowers and make their homes on our two acres of stony soil. Père watches them patiently. He uncovers their secrets and writes long books about their ways.

Père is very old. He is older than most children's fathers. He's already a grandfather. His sight is not as keen or his hearing as sharp as they once were, so my sisters and I lend him our eyes and our ears. In return, he teaches us about insects and lets us help him with his experiments. He also tells us stories about his life long ago in Avignon, when his first wife was alive and our half sisters and half brothers were all children. They are grown now and have children of their own.

When Père lived in Avignon, he was a schoolteacher. He taught physics and chemistry in the high school, but his favorite subject was natural history. And his favorite months of the year were July and August because he could spend the long summer days observing insects in the fields and hedgerows. Sometimes people thought he was simple-minded when they saw him sitting by the roadside for hours on end, seemingly staring at nothing. Once, when he was lying in a ditch taking in the details of a wasp household, he heard a voice say, "In the name of the law, I arrest you! Come along with me!"

Looking up, Père saw the angry face of the local game-keeper. Père tried to explain what he was doing.

"Pooh!" the man answered. "You'll never make me believe that you come here to roast in the sun to watch bees and wasps! I'll keep an eye on you, mark my word!"

He was sure that Père was a poacher out to steal a rabbit for his family's dinner.

The gamekeeper's warning didn't keep Père away from his insect studies. He still set out each morning at dawn, carrying a spade and a large umbrella. On his back was his collecting kit, which looked a lot like a poacher's bag. No wonder the gamekeeper thought that he was a suspicious-looking character. But the bag only held a magnifying lens, glass bottles, a trowel, a notebook, and tweezers.

The Two-Banded Scolia Wasp

Père always went to the same place that summer—a sandy bank in the woods, where he had noticed some little wasps cruising back and forth. They flew so low that they almost grazed the earth. Unfurling his umbrella, Père stuck it into the ground and sat down in its shade. He and the wasps were both interested in the same event. They were waiting for a young female wasp to dig her way out of the soil.

Some wasps, like yellow jackets, are social insects. They live in a nest as part of a large family, sharing the work of raising the young. Others, like the two-banded scolia, are solitary. But even solitary wasps go to a lot of trouble to provide for their children.

Père was curious about what young scolia wasps live on down in the soil. That was why his eyes never left the bank.

It was also why his spade was by his side. As soon as a scolia came up from the soil, he planned to dig out the shell of her cocoon, hoping that he would find some clue as to what she'd been eating.

Night after night, Père went home with nothing to show for his patience. Anyone else would have given up after a few days, but Père continued to keep watch for most of the summer. He was finally rewarded. A wasp popped out of the ground right before his eyes. She brushed away a few sand grains and flew off, followed by several males.

Père began to dig. Carefully sifting soil and bits of root between his fingers, he eventually found a split cocoon. It was attached to a fragment of empty skin. This was the clue he'd been hoping to find. The empty skin belonged to the grub on which the mother wasp had stuck an egg. The wasp larva then fed on the grub until it was ready to make its cocoon. Père could tell from the big jaws that the scrap of skin was from a beetle grub. But there wasn't enough of it for him to identify the beetle.

That was the only cocoon Père found that summer. Toward the end of August, the scolia wasps gave up flying over the bank. It would be useless to go on watching. Besides, it was time to go back to teaching school.

Twenty-three years have passed. Père now lives on the edge of the village of Sérignan on his own harmas. That's the name given in this part of Provence to dry land that grows little but thistles and thyme. Over the years, Père has

Le cycle de la vie de la guêpe.

cultivated the stony soil, planting trees and herbs to attract more insects. The harmas is surrounded by a high wall, so he can spend all day on his hands and knees looking at his insects without raising anyone's suspicions.

One hot August afternoon, Père again meets up with the two-banded scolia. And this time he finds out what kind of beetle the wasp larvae feed on—though some of the credit for the discovery really belongs to Favier, the gardener.

Favier is an old retired soldier who does odd jobs around the harmas. Père has asked him to move a pile of leaves and dirt away from the back wall because our dog, Tom, has been using the mound as a ramp when he decides to go out adventuring. Tom usually comes back with torn ears and a sad expression, so Père wants to keep him home.

Favier has moved only a few spadefuls of dirt when he shouts, "Here's a find, sir, a great find! Come and look!"

Père hurries over to see. The soil is swarming with white grubs. Père recognizes them. They are the larvae of the rose chafer beetle. Then he spots some little golden cocoons. He kneels down in the dirt. "These belong to my old friend scolia. Look, there's an adult!" He points to a little wasp tunneling through the dirt. Taking his magnifying lens from his pocket, he studies the cocoons and the empty skins next to them. Then he picks up a white beetle grub and examines its skin.

"What was once a difficult problem is now child's play!" he says with a smile. "Years ago I spent the whole summer trying to find out what scolia larvae eat. And now I have the answer at my own front door. They live on the grubs of the rose chafer beetle."

After everyone is in bed, Père goes up to his study at the back of the house and sits down at his desk. He can finally finish the chapter on the two-banded scolia wasp—the story that had its beginning twenty-three years before in the woods near Avignon.

Ground Wasps

Most entomologists study dead insects on pins. But not Père! He is curious about living insects. Insects are born knowing how to do many clever things by natural instinct. Some have the skill of a surgeon, others the skill of an engineer. Père is amazed at what insects can do. He is also surprised by how stupid they can be!

To learn more about instinct, Père often plays tricks on his insects. He calls his tricks experiments.

One bright September morning, Père, my sisters, and I are following the pebbly path through the harmas. The thistle heads have turned white and their seeds are drifting off, even though the air is almost still. About twenty yards in front of us, I see a tiny creature shoot up into the air, then another.

"Look, Père! Wasps! It's a wasps' nest for sure!"

We creep forward cautiously. We can now see a steady flow of yellow jackets zooming in and out of a small hole near the edge of the path. The wasps live together in a nest they have built in a burrow in the soil. Père tells us that the nest hangs like a paper lantern from the roof of the burrow, almost filling the cavity. The space around the nest serves as a wide street for worker wasps, who keep making the nest bigger and stronger.

The burrow was probably made by a mouse or a vole, but the wasps have enlarged it. As they dig, they carry crumbs of earth and rubbish outside, yet there's no pile of dirt to draw attention to the entrance. That's because the wasps fly some distance from home before dropping their load. The earth is scattered in all directions.

Wasps make paper by chewing wood fibers and mixing them with their saliva. The spongy walls of the nest are

made from overlapping sheets of paper with air spaces between. Inside the paper walls, layers of cells, or comb, are fastened to one another by a central pillar. The queen wasp lays an egg in each cell. When the eggs hatch, workers bring food to the young larvae. Wasp larvae eat, sleep, and grow while hanging upside down.

Père says that wasps are clever architects. They design

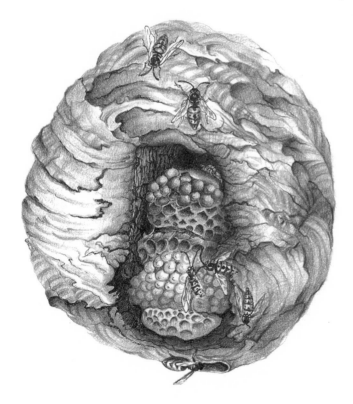

their nest so that it has the most room inside for the least amount of wrapper paper. The air spaces between the layers of paper provide good insulation. The tiers of cells are exactly the right distance apart to allow the nurse wasps to pass through to tend the young.

"Wasps have mastered the laws of geometry and physics," Père tells us. "But if they come up against an unexpected problem, can they find a solution?"

Père decides to play a trick on the wasps to find out.

The next morning, Père and I get up early and go back to the nest before the wasps are up and about. Père is carrying a glass bell jar. He sets it over the entrance to the nest.

The first wasps that come out fly upward, hit the glass wall, and drop to the ground. They pick themselves up and try again. Soon the jar is swarming with wasps. Some grow discouraged and return to the nest; others quickly take their place. Not a single wasp tries to dig its way out under the

jar, even though they know how to enlarge their underground cavity by digging.

Meanwhile, a few wasps who have spent the night outdoors return home. They can smell their nest down in the soil. When they find the entrance blocked by the jar, they buzz around in confusion. One of them, after a lot of hesitation, digs its way in. Others follow, and a passage is opened. Once the wasps are inside, Père closes the passage with earth. I want him to leave it open to see if any of the wasps that are buzzing about in the jar can discover the new exit, but Père says we must first find out if the wasps that dug their way into the nest will teach the others how to dig their way out.

We crouch beside the jar and wait for a long time, but nothing happens. The wasps keep on whirling around, bumping into the glass. Some finally collapse from heat or exhaustion.

Père says that the buzzing wasps are trapped by their instinct. Instinct tells them to fly up toward the sunshine. Even when they hit the glass, all they can do is to keep trying to fly upward, again and again. Because they cannot overcome their urge to aim for the light, they cannot solve the problem of how to escape. If only they would turn their back on the light for a while, they could dig their way to freedom!

Henri at School

Anna, Marie-Pauline, and I don't go to the village school. Père teaches us at home. In good weather, we do our lessons outdoors in the leafy shade of the big plane trees that grow in front of the house. Other times, we work in Père's study among cages of butterflies and crickets. When Père first went to school, he shared his classroom with chickens and pigs!

"Tell us about how you learned to read," Anna begs one morning.

We've heard the story before, but we close our exercise books and listen eagerly as Père tells us how he set off for school each morning, carrying a log of firewood. Classes were held in the schoolmaster's kitchen. The children's logs were for the master's fire, which both warmed the room

and cooked the pig food. Three big pots of potatoes and bran simmered on the hearth all day long, giving off puffs of steam. When the master wasn't looking, the boys sometimes helped themselves to a hot potato.

The master was mostly busy with the big boys, who sat around the table by the window, learning to write in flowing letters with goose-quill pens. Little Henri and the other six- and seven-year-olds sat on a bench against the opposite wall with their alphabet books open on their laps. Their eyes, however, were usually on the back door, which led to the yard where the hen scratched with her chicks and a dozen piglets wallowed in a stone trough. Sometimes, if the door wasn't properly latched, the piglets would push their way into the classroom, drawn by the smell of the potatoes cooking on the fire. They rubbed against the boys' legs and poked cold pink snouts into their hands, searching for scraps. The hen with her velvet-coated chicks came next. The master would then chase the animals back outside with a friendly flick of his handkerchief.

The little boys were supposed to be helping one another learn their letters, but none of them knew the alphabet, so the strange marks on the pages of their open books remained a mystery. Henri might never have learned to read if his father hadn't brought him a present from town. The present was a large colored poster divided into squares. In each square was an animal with a letter below it.

Henri pasted the poster to the wall beside his window. He liked to sit on the window seat and look out at the distant hills. Now when he sat there, he could also see his animal friends. One day, while he was looking at them, he realized that they were teaching him the sound of the letters in the mysterious alphabet book. Each letter made the sound of the beginning of the animal's name next to it. The animals on the poster carried him all the way through the alphabet.

Henri's father was so pleased that his son had finally learned his letters that he gave him a copy of La Fontaine's *Fables*. Here Henri found more of his favorite animals—crow, fox, magpie, frog, rabbit, dog, and cat. In this glorious

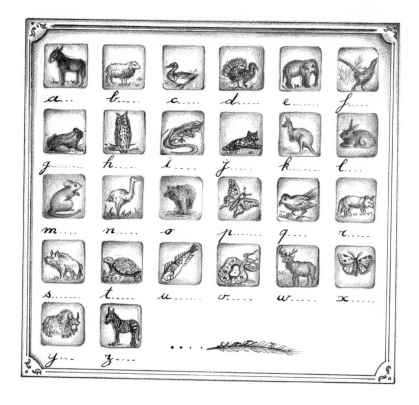

book, they talked the way people do. By putting the letters together, Henri could find out what they were saying.

My sisters and I can picture Père learning to read quite clearly, even though we've no idea how or when *we* learned *our* letters. Maybe that's because we've always been surrounded by books. Père didn't see a book until he was seven years old. His parents were so poor that when he was not much more than a baby he was sent to live with his grandparents. That made one less mouth for his parents to feed. His grandparents lived high in the hills in a farmhouse surrounded by mossy fens and heather with no neighbors for miles around. Père says they were people of the soil, whose quarrel with the alphabet was so great that they never opened a book. He lived with them until it was time for him to return to his parents' village and start school.

The Undertaker Beetle

Today, Père is reading about the strange ways of burying beetles. He's reading more to himself than to us, but we are all ears. These undertaker beetles go around the country-side digging graves for moles and mice. Their goal, however, is not to clean up the fields. The dead bodies provide food for their children. By burying the bodies, the beetles keep them safe from other scavengers.

The book claims that if the ground under the corpse is hard or stony, the beetle looks for an easier place to dig the grave. It then flies off and fetches some friends to help move the body. We can tell from Père's voice that he doubts if beetles are smart enough to plan ahead and work together like that. Nevertheless, burying beetles do have to overcome many difficulties. The soil under the body may be laced with the tough roots of couch grass. Sometimes a dead animal lands on a bramble bush when it is tossed from a trap or falls from a nest.

"If we had some burying beetles, we could see for ourselves how they go about solving these problems," Père says, closing the book. "But to attract burying beetles, we need some moles, and they don't live in the stony soil in the harmas. Where could we get a few dead moles?"

"From the man who brings us vegetables," Marie-Pauline suggests. "He traps them because they dig up his garden."

"Next time he comes, I'll ask him," Père says.

The vegetable man laughs when he hears Père's strange request, but he agrees to give us his dead moles. They come by twos, threes, and fours, packed in cabbage leaves in the bottom of the vegetable basket. The man isn't convinced that the moles are for beetle bait. He suspects that Père is going to turn the velvet skins into a winter waistcoat!

Soon we have thirty dead moles hidden under our rosemary bushes and in the lavender beds. Père and I make the rounds several times each day. We turn over the corpses in search of beetles that have flown in, attracted by the smell of rotting meat. Anna and Marie-Pauline refuse to help, but I don't mind. I've seen worse things than a dead mole.

We collect fourteen burying beetles in all. They are handsome insects. The tips of their antennae are decorated with little red tufts, and the black wing cases are banded with scarlet.

Père selects four beetles for his first experiment. He has

a cage ready—a large clay planter filled with light, sandy soil and covered with wire mesh. A dead mole lies on the mound of soil. To keep the mole safe from our cat, Ginger, he suspends the cage in a tripod made from long bamboo poles.

We watch Père place the beetles in the cage. Right away, they dig down into the soil under the mole. Soon the mole starts to tremble and shake as if it were alive. Every now and then one of the beetles pops out, takes a look at the body, and then goes back to work. As the beetles scoop the sandy soil out from under the mole, it slowly sinks into the ground. The mole appears to be burying itself!

Three days later, Père and I do a little digging in the cage. We find poor mole deep in the soil. He has lost his sleek velvet coat and is now a greenish color and smells really bad. He is not a pleasant sight. Père congratulates me for being the only one with the courage to watch, so I stay and

help him look for the beetles. At first we find only two—a male and a female. Then we discover the others near the edge of the pot, close to the surface of the soil.

In spite of their gruesome way of life, burying beetles are better fathers than most insects. The male helps the female prepare a place for their young. Very few male insects do that.

Père is now ready to see if beetles really drag the body to softer soil when the original place is too hard to dig. He puts a brick in the middle of the clay pot and covers it with a thin layer of dirt. The rest of the soil in the pot is light and sandy. Then Père lays a dead mouse above the brick. He chooses a small mouse this time instead of a mole so that it will be easier for the beetles to move.

At seven o'clock in the morning, Père places seven beetles in the cage. We had breakfast early so that we'll have plenty of time to watch what happens. Right away, three beetles slip under the mouse. The mouse begins to move. It's still jerking around two hours later. We can see the beetles working in the thin layer of soil that covers the brick. They dig with their feet. To move the body, they turn over onto their backs, grab the animal's hair in their claws, and push with their heads.

Finally, it seems to occur to one of the beetles that they aren't making much progress. He pops up and studies the corpse. Then he wanders about for a little while, aimlessly scratching the soil. He goes back to the mouse, and the body begins to jerk toward the edge of the brick. I'm sure he has figured out a way to solve the problem. But then the

body moves back from the edge of the brick. For the next three hours the beetles jerk the body about in a three-way tug of war.

Mother calls us in for lunch, but now two beetles are taking a fresh look at the problem. They scout the whole cage and make a few trial borings in the soil close to the side of the pot. Back they go to the mouse again. I'm ready to eat, but Père is sure that this time the beetles know what they're doing. The mouse inches steadily toward the place where they were digging. The burial is finally under way at one o'clock.

Père admits that the beetles were smart enough to move a body to lighter soil. But he points out that they didn't prepare the grave ahead of time. He thinks they need to feel the weight of the animal on their backs before they get serious about digging. Nor did they recruit other beetles to help. Any other beetles that show up probably do so because they smell the corpse and not because they've been invited by the original beetles.

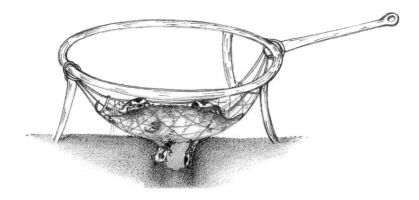

The following day, we present our beetles with new problems. Père wants to see what they do when the corpse is caught up in tough grass or roots. He tells me to ask Favier for some strips of the raffia he uses for tying up plants in the garden. Raffia's a lot like tough blades of couch grass. Next Père sends me to the kitchen to borrow an iron trivet from the range.

We make a little hammock out of the raffia. Then we put a dead mole in it and hang it from the trivet. It barely touches the soil. The beetles don't take long to realize that the mole isn't sinking into the hole they are digging under it. They immediately snip through the bottom of the hammock with their scissorlike mandibles.

When we tie a mole to the trivet by its legs instead of making a hammock, the beetles take longer to figure out what's wrong. But once again, they free the mole by cutting through the raffia.

Next Père places a mouse among the twigs of a thyme plant. This time the beetles climb a twig and push against the mouse with their backs. While doing so, they make such a commotion that the whole plant begins to shake. The mouse falls to the ground, and the beetles go to work and bury it.

I think that these beetles are very smart, but Père says that—like the wasps—they work within the framework of their instinct. The problems we gave them are similar to those they come up against in nature. Faced with a new problem, such as escaping from the cage, they cannot solve it. When we place a dead mouse outside the cage, not one beetle thinks of tunneling its way under the wire fence to reach it.

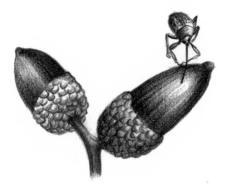

Acorn Elephants

Anna, Marie-Pauline, and I have spent the rainy after-noon indoors, sitting close to the fire, doing our lessons. I've been reading a chemistry textbook that Père wrote a long time ago. In the book two boys, named Emile and Jules, do all sorts of experiments with the help of their uncle, who is a chemist. Emile and Jules are my older brothers. I wonder how they felt when they met themselves in the pages of Père's book.

The October wind, moaning around the chimney pots, sends puffs of smoke into the room. The table is already set for dinner. Mother has just lit the lamp, which makes it sud-denly very dark outside. Where is Père? The insect season is over, so what has made him lose track of time?

A few minutes later, the door bursts open and in he

comes, shaking the rain off his coat. He is carrying a bouquet of oak twigs, heavy with acorns.

"Where have you been?" Mother asks. Worry gives an edge of sharpness to her voice.

"Elephant hunting," Père answers.

"Did you bring one home?" little Anna wants to know, her blue eyes wide with excitement.

"Of course!" Père says. "Come and see!"

Dinner is forgotten as we all troop up to his study to be introduced to Père's elephant. Only Anna is surprised when the elephant turns out to be a beetle. Even though it's a small beetle, we can see how it got its name. The acorn elephant's snout is so long that it has to hold it straight out so as not to trip over it.

"The first one I found was using its long snout to drill a hole in an acorn," Père tells us. "I supposed that it was preparing a place for its egg. I wanted to make sure, but the wind was blowing the branch about so much that it was hard to watch the beetle. I finally had to cut the branch and move it to a more sheltered spot. The beetle didn't seem to notice. It kept on drilling, walking in semicircles, using its snout like an awl. When its nose was completely buried in the acorn, it rested for a while and then pulled it out."

"Then it turned around and laid an egg in the hole," Marie-Pauline said.

Père shook his head. "It just wandered off among the withered leaves! All that drilling for nothing. And all my waiting for nothing. But I've brought some beetles home so that we can learn about their ways in comfort."

Père puts the oak twigs in two jars and covers them with a dome of wire mesh so that the beetles cannot fly away. He places the cage near the window, where it will be well lighted.

Two days later, a female begins to bore into an acorn. This is no easy matter. The little beetle has to point her drill-nose straight down, balancing on her hind feet and on the tips of her wing covers in order to get enough height. Sticky pads on the bottom of her feet help her hold her position on the smooth, slippery nut.

We take turns watching her at work. It's my shift and almost dark when the hole is finally as deep as her snout. I call to Père. But again he is disappointed. The beetle pulls out her snout and wanders off, abandoning the hole that she worked on for eight long hours.

Finally Père does see a beetle turn around and lay an egg in the hole she has drilled. But he's still puzzled by why so many beetles abandon the holes. The next day, he tells us to dress warmly. We're going to the oak woods to look for acorns that have been punctured by elephant beetles. Once we know what to look for, it's not hard to find acorns with a tiny needle prick in them. The little beetles have been busy.

Marie-Pauline finds a dead elephant beetle and calls us over to see it. It died with its nose stuck in the nut and its feet in the air. Père says its feet must have slipped while it was digging. Its snout straightened, so that it ended up in this strange position, unable to move and unable to eat. Père calls it an industrial accident. Like people in factories, these beetles can be victims of their tools.

When Père cuts open the pierced acorns, he finds that some are empty, while others contain an egg or a newly hatched larva. The egg is always at the far end of the tunnel, where the tissue is moist and soft. In acorns where there's no egg, the tissue is hard.

"I think the beetle must bore into the nut to find tissue that is soft enough for the new larva to eat," Père explains. "She's like a mother testing the temperature of the broth before offering the spoon to her baby. If the food isn't exactly right, the beetle abandons the nut and goes off to look for another. But now we have a new problem. How does the egg always end up at the far end of the tunnel?"

"It falls to the bottom," I say quickly. I don't see the problem.

Père shakes his head. "Sometimes the beetles bore sideways or even straight up. Besides, the tunnel is so full of shavings that there isn't room for the egg to fall."

"Maybe she pushes it into the hole with her elephant's snout," Marie-Pauline suggests.

"We shall have to watch and find out," Père answers.

Back in the study, we see another beetle lay an egg. As soon as she walks away, Père dissects the acorn. The egg is at the bottom of the hole. Other insects, such as the grasshopper that lays its eggs in the earth, have a swordlike egg-laying tool called an ovipositor. The elephant beetle doesn't appear to have such a tool, but when Père dissects a beetle, he finds something that takes his breath away. Inside the abdomen is an ovipositor that is exactly the same length as the beetle's snout. It is like a plunger that carries the egg to the bottom of the tunnel, and then is drawn back into the body. It would be too hard for the little beetle to get around with a long snout at one end and a long ovipositor at the other, so she carries her egg-laying tool inside her body.

Père sits down at his desk. He has something new to write about.

The Caterpillar Parade

Every winter, groups of caterpillars set up camp in the pine trees in the harmas. They spin tents of silk to keep out the wind and rain. In the evening, they leave their tents and go foraging for pine needles. These caterpillars have big appetites and can do a lot of damage. Usually Père protects his trees by knocking down the tents with a long forked stick, but this year he has made a pact with the pine caterpillars. They will be his "children of winter" and can live in his trees, eating all the needles they want. In return, they must tell him their story.

We get to stay up late to watch the caterpillars. They do their eating under cover of darkness. When they leave the tent, they travel together in a long line. The first caterpillar out of the tent tosses its head from side to side, trying to decide on the best route, and the others follow blindly, each head touching the tail in front of it. No spaces are left between. The lead caterpillar dribbles an invisible silk thread for the next one to follow. The second caterpillar adds to the silken roadway. So does the third, and the fourth, and on down the line. When the last caterpillar has passed along the road, all those invisible threads add up to a shining white ribbon.

On reaching a branch with lots of needles, the caterpillars fan out and get down to the serious business of eating. After a while, full stomachs and the falling temperature tell them it's time to return to camp. They follow their individual pathways back to the common road. Whichever caterpillar finds itself at the head of the line leads the others home.

In stormy weather, the caterpillars stay snug inside their

tent; in mild weather, they sometimes go exploring in the daytime. Once we counted three hundred caterpillars winding down a tree trunk and marching across the ground. Père thinks that they may have been scouting out places where they could spin their cocoons later on. After a while, the leader looped around in a winding curve until it found the silk road to take the procession back to the tent. Caterpillars never do an "about turn" on their roadway. The leader just wanders about until it finds the road again. Sometimes they don't make it home before dark. During the coldest part of the night, the caterpillars huddle together until the temperature rises again.

Père brings some branches with tents on them into the greenhouse. He plants them in tubs of sand and places them on a low shelf near a big potted palm. The caterpillars begin to parade all over the place. Père wonders what tricks he can play on them. Removing the leader doesn't bother them at all. The second in line immediately takes over and chooses the route. Breaking the silk road doesn't upset them either, except that there are now two parades instead of one. If the second parade stumbles onto the path of the first one, they join up again. The leader becomes a follower.

The caterpillars like to parade up and down the big palm pot. This gives Père an idea, but he has to wait for the right conditions. His patience is soon rewarded. One morning in late January, just before noon, a column of caterpillars climbs the pot and the leader makes its way around the cir-

cular lip with all the other caterpillars following. It takes
fifteen minutes for the leader to complete the circle. Père
quickly brushes away the caterpillars that are still coming
up, so that the ones on the top of the pot form an uninter-
rupted circle. Each caterpillar is now a follower, adding its
dribble of thread to the silken road. There is no longer a
leader.

It's lunchtime, but none of us wants to leave. We have to
see what's going to happen next.

"The procession will go on turning for some time, for an
hour, two hours perhaps," Père guesses. "Then they'll see
their mistake and head for home."

We grow tired of watching before the caterpillars grow
tired of walking. Père times them. They are traveling at

about $3^{1}/_{2}$ inches a minute. They slow down as the temperature drops. By ten o'clock in the evening, they're hardly moving at all. Grazing time has arrived for the other caterpillars, but the ones on the pot go hungry.

At dawn, they are lined up as they were yesterday, but they're not moving. However, when the temperature rises, they start off again, following the silk road. We can't believe it. Anna, Marie-Pauline, and I take turns checking on them.

The next night is very cold. The rosemary sparkles with frost and the garden pond is skimmed with ice. Although the caterpillars in the greenhouse have some protection, we can tell that they had a bad night. They're huddled in two groups. Père predicts that they'll break free from the silk road. As soon as it's warm enough, the two groups begin to move, each with its own leader. Both leaders follow the road. By the time all the caterpillars have taken their places, the circle is complete again and everyone is a follower, going nowhere.

The fourth day is uneventful. On the fifth day, a few caterpillars break away and go on an excursion down inside the pot. They finally rejoin the others. The following day is much warmer. A few brave souls make their way down the outside of the pot and escape the circle. Two days later, on the eighth day, the rest of the caterpillars, singly or in groups, follow the trail of the pioneers. By sunset they are all back in their tent.

Père turns the caterpillar parade into an arithmetic lesson. "How far did they travel?" he asks. "They were on the pot for seven days and nights. Let's say they rested half the time."

At a speed of $3\frac{1}{2}$ inches a minute, the caterpillars covered 1,470 feet. We measure the circumference of the pot. It is $52\frac{1}{2}$ inches. Père is amazed to learn that the caterpillars circled the vase 336 times!

Why would they risk starvation rather than leave the road, we wonder.

"The silk road is their lifeline," Père explains. "Without the instinct to follow the silk road, pine caterpillars could not survive. They browse at night, so they must find their way back to the tent in the darkness. The tent provides protection against snow, gales, and icy fogs. All winter long, they strengthen and enlarge it. One caterpillar can't make a tent on its own. The silk thread is more than a road. It is what holds the community together."

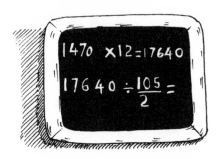

Lucie and the Ants

After the supper dishes are cleared away, we pull our chairs close to the dining room fire. "Can you think of any other insects that parade through the harmas?" Père asks.

"Red ants!" Marie-Pauline and I answer together.

In summer, we sometimes see long columns of ants threading their way through the grass, over leaf piles, and across paths. They are looking for slaves to take home to do all the work. If these raiding parties find a black-ant nest, they swarm through the entrance and head straight for the nursery. When they come back out, each red ant has a white-clad baby in its jaws. Meanwhile, the black ants scuttle around helplessly, trying to save their children, but they are no match for the fierce red ants. The stolen babies are actually cocoons. When the adults emerge in their new surroundings, they meekly take over all the housekeeping duties for the red ants. They even feed them.

"Tell us the story about Lucie marking the trail," Anna says.

Lucie is my oldest sister Antoine's daughter. She's Père's granddaughter and my niece. She was fourteen when I was born, and is now grownup and has a baby of her own. Ours is a hard family to sort out!

Père goes over to the shelves and selects one of his own books. "Lucie was a great one for stories when she was your age," he says. "She liked to hear about the theft of the white-clothed babies. We once witnessed a great battle between the red and black ants."

When Père returns to his seat by the fire, he opens the book to the chapter on red ants. "When the ants return to their nest, they retrace every twist and turn of their outward journey," he explains. "They meander all over the harmas, never taking short cuts, even though they are now

weighed down by the stolen babies. People say they follow an invisible road, guided by their sense of smell, but I was not convinced. I was looking for an answer to that question, so I asked Lucie to keep watch for the next raiding party."

In his book, Père calls Lucie his "six-year-old colleague," even though she was really just his helper. One day, while he was spinning out his daily quota of words, there came a great banging at the study door.

"It's Lucie!" a voice shouted. "Come quick! The red ants have gone into the black ants' house. Do come quick!"

"Do you know the road they took?" Père asked.

"Yes, I marked it."

"Marked it? How?"

"I did what Hop-o'-My-Thumb did," Lucie explained proudly. "I scattered little white stones along the road."

Père sent Lucie running to the house to find a broom. By the time she came back, the red ants, each with a stolen baby in its jaws, were already heading for home along the path she'd marked with the white stones. Père swept the path clean a few yards ahead of the column. When the first ants reached the place where he'd swept, they became confused. Some explored the edge of the swept area and finally joined up with their original path. Others walked straight across. Père tried sweeping a few more sections. Each time, after some hesitation, the ants rejoined the trail on the other side.

Could their waving antennae pick up the smell of the trail even after it had been disturbed by all that sweeping?

The next time Lucie reported a raid, Père washed a three-foot area of the path with water from the garden hose. He left the hose running. It was fifteen minutes before the ants returned. That should be long enough to wash away any lingering scent. When the first ants arrived, Père slowed the water to a trickle so as not to drown them. The ants were again confused. Some tried to cross the river on stones sticking above the water. A few lucky ones were able to use dry olive leaves as rafts. Others fell into the water and were swept downstream. Lucie wanted to rescue them, but Père said she must let them find their own way home, if they could. Lucie was glad to see that no matter what happened, the red ants didn't abandon the stolen babies. Père still wasn't sure if the ants were finding their way by their sense of smell or by memory. He decided to play more tricks on them to find out.

I'm surprised when Père reaches the end of the chapter

and closes the book. Instead of listening, I've been thinking about Lucie helping Père with his experiments all those years ago just as Anna and Marie-Pauline and I do now. I wonder if he'll ever write about us in his books.

Henri and the Saxicola

Mother is also thinking about Lucie. Instead of chasing us off to bed, she turns to Père and says, "Lucie would still fret over a lost ant. Her feeling for insects must go back to that summer she spent here with you on the harmas."

"I don't think that's something you learn," Père answers. "It's something you're born with. I can still recall the excitement of my first insect discovery. I must have been about five years old. I was standing in the doorway of my grandparents' cottage at dusk and I could hear a jingling sound in the bushes. Was it a little bird chirping in its nest? Even though I greatly feared the wolf that might come out of the woods, I crept over to the bushes to look. The jingling immediately stopped. I tried again the next evening, and the evening after. This time I was successful. Whoosh!

A grab of my hand and I had the singer. It wasn't a bird but a grasshopper! So I learned, from my own observation, that grasshoppers sing."

"Did your grandparents foster your interest?" Mother asks.

Père laughs and says, "Not at all! Grandfather would have been dumbfounded had he known that, in the distant future, one of his own family would spend all his days studying such worthless animals. 'The idea of wasting one's time with that nonsense!' he would have thundered. Once childhood's games were past, one shouldn't be rearing grasshoppers or digging up dung beetles! Grandmother would have felt the same way. Though I do think she gave me my fondness for stories. I remember how we children formed a circle around her and listened to her tales with eager ears. Tales that made our flesh creep. The wolf played a part, and the dragon, and the serpent."

"What about your parents?" Mother persists. "Did they encourage you?"

"Their minds were also taken up with practical matters," Père answers. "Like trying to keep food on the table. Not long after I went back to live with them, they decided to raise ducks to make a little extra money. When the ducklings outgrew their tub of water in the yard, it became my job to take them to the stream. While the ducklings splashed about, I chased the long-legged bugs that walk on water and examined the little creatures that live under rocks in stone houses. In a tree overhanging the stream, I caught a blue beetle that shone like a jewel. I put it into an empty snail shell, plugged it with a leaf, and stuffed it in my pocket. Soon my pocket was bulging with other treasures—a stone that was hollow and shone with crystals, and a rock that looked like a little ram's horn. On the way home, my pocket ripped under the weight of all my finds.

"My parents met me at the door. 'You rascal!' my father said, when he saw the damage. 'I sent you to mind the ducks and you spend your time picking up stones as though there weren't enough of them around here! Make haste and throw them away!'

" 'A nice thing bringing up children to see them turn out so badly!' my mother added. 'Green stuff I don't mind; it does for the rabbits. But stones, which ruin your pockets; poisonous animals, which'll sting your hand—what good are they to you, silly? There's no doubt about it; someone has thrown a spell over you!' "

When Père reaches the end of his story, Anna, Marie-Pauline, and I are indignant. How could this grandmother (whom we never met) scold little Henri like that?

Père just laughs and tells us another story.

From his window, he could see a steep hill with a row of trees on the very top. Sometimes the trees stood still and upright against the blue sky. Other times they turned their backs to the wind and danced like madmen. On those days they seemed as though they might uproot themselves and take flight.

Henri made up his mind to climb the hill and visit the

trees. Partway up, he spotted a bird's nest on the ground, half-hidden by a rock. It was the first nest he'd ever found. In it were six blue eggs. He lay down in the grass and stared at them while the mother bird flew anxiously from stone to stone. A plan was running through little Henri's head—a plan that Père said was worthy of a beast of prey. In two weeks, he'd come back and collect the nestlings before they could fly away. In the meantime, he'd take one of the pretty blue eggs as a trophy. He placed it on a bed of moss and set off for home, carrying it carefully in his open hand. He would visit the trees another day.

At the bottom of the hill, Henri met the parish priest.

"What have you there, my boy?" he asked.

Henri showed him the blue egg.

"Ah!" said the priest. "A saxicola's egg! Where did you get it?"

"Up there, Father, under a stone. By chance, I found a nest that I was not looking for. There were six eggs in it. I took one of them—here it is—and I am waiting for the rest to hatch. I shall go back for the others when the young birds have their quill feathers."

"You mustn't do that, my little friend," the priest replied. "You must not rob the mother of her brood. Be a good boy, now, and don't touch the nest."

Henri promised.

He learned two things from his conversation with the priest. The first was that he shouldn't plunder birds' nests. The other was that animals have names just as we do. But why was it called a saxicola? (Years later, when he studied Latin, he found out that saxicola means "inhabitant of the rocks.") Did plants have names as well, he wondered. And insects? Now he wanted a name for everything he found.

My sisters and I sit quietly, hoping that this will lead to another story about little Henri, but before Père gets started, Mother says it's time for bed.

The Feast

It's Shrove Tuesday, the day before Lent, and Père has planned a special dinner. We are having guests. Père has two friends in the village, who sometimes visit him on Sunday afternoons, especially in winter when the north wind is blowing. They are Jullian, the village schoolmaster, and Marius Guigne. We are secretly in awe of Marius. He is blind, but he handles carpenters' tools with more skill than most sighted people do. Père and his two friends sit by a roaring fire and talk about everything. The only forbidden topic is politics.

It was during one of those afternoon discussions that plans were made for today's feast. The schoolmaster told Père that the Romans used to eat the cossus grub that lives in oak trees. It was considered a great delicacy. Père says that we must try them when they are in season. So today we are all seated around the table with cossus grubs roasting on the grill. They sizzle and turn golden. Little spurts of flame spring up as the fat drips down onto the hot coals. No one knows what sauce the Romans served with the grubs. We are having them with a pinch of salt.

Père offers the platter to the schoolmaster first. He selects the smallest grub and is in no hurry to start eating. Anna and Marie-Pauline giggle nervously as Père serves them two grubs apiece. Marius dives in without any hesitation. For once, not being able to see is an advantage.

I follow Père's example and stab the roast grub with my fork. It is juicy and tender. Père smacks his lips and says his grub tastes like burnt almonds. Mother can detect a hint of

vanilla flavor. We all agree that there's nothing wrong with eating grubs. But we are relieved when Père says that they are too rare to become a regular part of our diet.

While we're eating our unusual dinner, Père tells us that for a few years his father tried to earn his living as a cook. When Père was ten, Grandfather moved the family about thirty miles to the city of Rodez, where he ran a café. Although Père missed the open countryside, the move gave him the chance to get a good education. He was allowed to attend Rodez secondary school for free by becoming a server in the chapel. Père was always tongue-tied with shyness when he and the other three servers marched, two by two, to the middle of the sanctuary. He was never sure when to ring his bell, and he always left it to the others to recite the Latin chants. However, he soon mastered Latin at school. The Roman poet Virgil wrote about the things in nature that Père loved—bees, cicadas, crows, turtledoves, nanny goats, and golden broom.

Jullian interrupts Père's story with a stream of Latin verse. Our Roman meal ends with the schoolmaster and Père trying to outdo each other in showing how much of Virgil's poetry they can remember.

The Scorpion Theater

The glass cage that sits on the bench in Père's study appears to be empty, but under each of the pieces of broken flowerpot that are lined up along the sides of the cage lurks a scorpion, the color of dead straw. They are big creatures, about three inches long. A scorpion is an arachnid, a relative of the spider, and is armed with strong claws and a curved tail with a poisonous sting at the tip. It has no neck. The scorpion's head and body are fused together. Even though it has eight eyes, it moves like a blind man, feeling its way.

On April evenings, between the hours of seven and nine o'clock, the scorpions leave their flowerpot homes and join together in a mad scorpion dance. It's as good as a performance at the theater, and we come running from all corners

of the house to watch. Even Tom and Ginger join us, though they mostly curl up and sleep at our feet. A lantern hung close to the glass palace lets us see the magical drama. The scorpions are drawn to the light and pass solemnly to and fro, coming and going. Some dance face to face, claw to claw, but fly apart the moment they touch as if they'd burned their fingers. Others emerge from the shadows and glide out to join the crowd on the stage.

Sometimes there's such a tangle of swarming legs, snapping claws, and clashing tails that we think we are watching a battle to the death. But then the group separates, everyone rests, and there isn't a wound among them. Now we see two wrestlers standing on their heads like acrobats, their tails held straight up. Then the pyramid falls, and each one hurries away.

It's hard to tell if the wrestlers are rival males or a courting couple.

Later, a new drama unfolds in the scorpion palace that leads us to think that a scorpion declares his love by standing on his head! We find a mother scorpion carrying eggs on the underside of her abdomen. When the eggs hatch, the mother presses her claws close to the ground so that the tiny creatures can hoist themselves up and climb onto her back. They stay there for eight days without moving. Then they cast their skins and we can now make out their tiny claws and curved tails. They run and play around on their mother's back for the next two weeks. Then it's time for them to venture out on their own.

Père gives the grown scorpions beetles to eat, but he cannot provide live food for such tiny creatures, so we must say goodbye to them. He sets them free on a rock-strewn slope where the sun is hot. We're sad to see them go. Not all of them will survive, but Père tells us that they're better off taking their chance out in the world than starving in a glass palace.

The Great Peacock Moth

By nine o'clock in the evening in early May, it's dark outside. One night, when I go upstairs to get ready for bed, I'm in for a great surprise. My room has been raided by giant moths! They are streaming in through the open window and fluttering madly against the furniture and ceiling.

Scrambling up on the bed, I trap a moth against the wall. It struggles softly in my hand. After lodging it in an empty birdcage, I go after another. In the excitement of the chase, I send a chair flying and bump into the table.

"Come quick, Père!" I yell. "Come and see these moths as big as birds! The room is full of them!"

Père has heard the ruckus and is already on his way. By now I have trapped four moths.

Right away, Père knows the answer to the moth inva-

sion. "Leave your cage, Paul, and come with me," he says. "We will see something interesting!"

Père lights the way with his candle. I follow him down the stairs and through the kitchen. Giant moths have taken over the whole house. When we reach the study, we are met by an unforgettable sight. It's like stepping into a wizard's cave, awhirl with bats. The center of the activity is a wire cage sitting on Père's worktable. With a soft flick-flack of wings, moths mob the cage, jostling for a place close to it. Some fly up to the ceiling and then are drawn back to the cage again.

Père explains the cause of the excitement. This morning a female peacock moth emerged from a cocoon that had been lying on the table. He had no plans for the moth, but out of habit he placed the wire cage over it. The invaders are male moths that have flown through the darkness to pay court to the imprisoned princess. Some are confused by our light. They swoop toward the candle and their great flapping wings put out the flame. They land on our shoulders and cling to our clothes.

I reach out for Père's hand.

Around ten-thirty the moths stop coming. Père counts twenty in the study, though it seems like more. If we add the moths in the other rooms, there must be forty. Our prisoner has attracted forty suitors.

How did they know that the female was here? How did they find their way to our house in the dark? Père says that he thinks they must be guided by their sense of smell. But

how do they pick up the scent of the female moth? Is that
the purpose of their big, feathery antennae?

Père decides to find out.

The next day, most of the moths have left through the
open window, but Père finds eight males resting on the
frame of the second window, which is closed. With a sharp
pair of scissors, he snips off their antennae. I shut my eyes,
but Père says he doesn't think that they feel anything. They
don't flutter their wings or give any sign of discomfort. He
releases them outside.

After dark, we move the female in her cage to the porch
at the other end of the house. Soon the suitors arrive. We're
ready for them. We catch them in butterfly nets and put
them in a room off the porch. We don't want to keep catch-
ing the same moths again and again. We trap twenty-five
males in a couple of hours. One has no antennae.

We repeat the experiment the following evening, moving the moth to a new place. This time not one of the males

with missing antennae shows up. Maybe the hornless males didn't go courting because they were ashamed of how they looked. Père comes up with another way of marking males so that he will know them later. He shaves a little fur off the thorax and then releases them. The girls and I choose another hiding place for the female. Of the twenty moths we catch, only two have shaved fur.

Père is discouraged. He has not really proved that the male moths use their antennae to find a mate. Most of the males didn't come back the second night with or without antennae. He thinks that the reason they don't come back is that they don't live very long. Unlike some other kinds of butterflies and moths, the peacock doesn't have a coiled tongue with which it can sip nectar from flowers. Peacock moths do not eat as adults, so the males live for only a day or two. The female, who does nothing but wait, lives several days longer.

Père thinks up another experiment to test their sense of smell. He puts the female under a glass bell jar. No suitors arrive. But when he hides her in a cupboard inside a hatbox with a lid that isn't tight, males arrive and beat against the door with their wings as if they were knocking for permission to enter! The males must be attracted by the female's scent. But how could a scent that none of us can smell draw in males from miles away?

Our princess lives for eight days. This isn't nearly long enough to answer all Père's questions. He begins to make plans for next year. He'll need more cocoons, but they aren't easy to find because we have no almond trees, and that's what the caterpillars feed on. He'll offer the village children a sou for each cocoon they bring him. Though Père says that what he really needs is a daytime-flying species. It's hard to observe the peacock moths without a lamp, but to the males a shining light is even more attractive than the princess in the cage.

Anna, Marie-Pauline, and I do not think that a daytime moth would be half so interesting. We like playing hide-and-seek with the great peacocks in the dark.

The Leaf-Cutter Bee

The lilac and rose leaves in the harmas are riddled with small holes. Some are perfectly round; others are oval. Père tells us that the holes are the work of the leaf-cutter bee. She cuts them with her scissorlike mandibles. The oval pieces are fashioned into thimble-shaped cells, which the little bee places in a borrowed tunnel made in the soil by an earthworm or in a tree trunk by a wood-boring beetle. The bee furnishes each cell with pollen on which she lays a single egg. Then she seals the cell with a round lid. She adds several more lids and then makes another cell. She keeps on working until the tunnel is full.

One evening, while we are sitting by the kitchen fire, Père poses a problem.

"Suppose there was a pot that you use every day, whose lid has just been broken. It was knocked down by the cat playing on the shelves. Tomorrow is market day and you're going to town to buy the week's provisions. Which of you, relying solely on memory, would undertake to bring back a lid that is exactly the right size for the pot? It must be neither too small nor too large."

We agree that it would be hard to do. Marie-Pauline says she would use a piece of string to measure the width of the lid. I think I could pick out a lid that might do, but it would be a matter of luck if it was exactly the right size.

Père then tells us that the leaf-cutter bee is cleverer than we are when it comes to housekeeping matters. She has no mental picture of her pot, because she made it in the dark of her tunnel. Yet, when she is far from home, she manages to cut out a top that fits her jar exactly.

"Maybe she first cuts a piece larger than she needs and gnaws away the surplus," Mother suggests.

Père shakes his head. "The insect can't go back to cutting once the disk is detached from the leaf. A tailor would spoil his cloth if he did not have the support of a table while cut-

ting out pieces for a coat. The little bee would do equally bad work if the leaf was not supported by the plant. The bee stands on top of the leaf while she cuts out the lid. She then flies off, carrying it against her chest. Each cell is sealed with as many as ten pieces, with the undersurface of the leaf always facing down. If the bee stopped to trim the lid, surely some of the time it would get turned over."

"The bee knows how to make it exactly the right size by instinct," I tell Père. "The same way that wasps know how wide to make the passageways between the cells."

Père smiles. "You're right, Paul!" he says. "Though the leaf-cutter bee certainly deserves credit for being a hard worker. I once found a tunnel that contained 17 cells that were the work of a single bee. An average of 42 pieces of leaf went into making each cell, and then the bee barricaded the tunnel with another 350 pieces of leaf. So how many trips did she make to furnish the tunnel?"

I'm worn out by the time I come up with the answer, but I'm not so tired as the little bee must have been after making a total of 1,064 journeys!

The Sisyphus Dung Beetle

Père has announced that today is a holiday. The blackboard gets a rest! We are going on a hunting expedition to look for Sisyphus beetles. We're so eager to set out that we don't bother to eat. After we've walked for an hour or two, Père opens his knapsack and brings out crusty bread and apples. Breakfast tastes better served in the shade of a hedgerow among the May flowers. While we munch on our apples, Père tells us about the beetles and how they got their name.

Sisyphus is about the size of a cherry pit and is the smallest and most industrious of a group of beetles known as dung beetles. Dung beetles get their nourishment from animal droppings. Sisyphus prefers sheep dung. That's why we're heading for the sheep pastures at the foot of the mountains.

When Sisyphus beetles are ready to raise a family, the male and the female work together, shaping a piece of dung into a ball about the size of a pea. Then they bury it to provide food for their offspring. But first they roll it about to give it a hard crust so that it won't dry out in hot weather. The female walks in front, dragging the ball backwards. The male brings up the rear, pushing it with his back legs. Because the beetles are both facing backwards, they can't see where they're going. They constantly trip over obstacles. If they choose a slope that's too steep, ball and beetles all come rolling down. The beetles pick themselves up, shake themselves off, and try again.

It's this habit of rolling balls about that gives these beetles their name. Sisyphus was a character in Greek mythology who was so deceitful that he even tried to cheat Death. As a punishment, he was sentenced to roll a huge rock uphill forever. When he reached the summit, the rock rolled down and he had to start again.

Père says he knows just how Sisyphus felt. For all his life he has carried the burden of poverty on his shoulders. No sooner does he get his load balanced than it rolls downhill again. For twenty years, he taught science in the boys' high school at Avignon without ever getting a raise in salary. Even though his students did well, his superiors didn't like his teaching methods. The final straw was when he admitted girls to his evening science classes. He lost his job. He gave up teaching and moved to Orange, where he wrote textbooks on all sorts of subjects—chemistry, mushrooms, volcanoes, butterflies, and bees. One day, for no reason, the landlord cut down the avenue of plane trees in front of Père's house. That was too much for Père. He decided he must find a place of his own, so he moved to the nearby village of Sérignan. On the harmas, he has peace and quiet, but he still worries about providing for his family. He works hard, writing far into the night, long after we are all in bed.

When we reach the sheep pastures near the mountains, the hunt for Sisyphus begins. Père tells us that the beetles spend the day inside cakes of sun-dried dung. I seem to have an instinct for likely hiding places. In no time we have collected six couples. Père's earlier worries are now forgotten. With twelve Sisyphus beetles, he is rich beyond his wildest ambitions!

Back in his study, Père provides his beetles with a bed of sand and a diet to their taste. He covers the cage with a

wire-mesh dome. Soon one pair of beetles feel sufficiently at home to start a family. We watch them make their ball of dung and roll it around. The mother tries to climb up the inside of the roof, fixing her claws in the wire and dragging the ball upward. The father hangs on, adding his weight, and both beetles take a tumble. They pick themselves up and try again.

Finally they decide it's time to bury the ball. While the mother beetle digs a pit, the father entertains us by juggling the ball between his hind legs. Père imagines that he is bragging about the beautiful loaf he has made. He is holding it up so that we can see the fine, hard crust that protects the soft dough inside. He's telling us that he has baked the loaf for his children!

When the pit is deep enough, the beetles carefully roll the ball into it. Then they go back to digging until they and the ball disappear from sight. Later, Père unearths a buried pellet and finds that it is no longer round. It is now shaped like a tiny pear. While the mother was underground, she re-worked the ball, giving it a narrow neck at one end, where she laid a single egg. If she laid the egg in the middle of the dung ball, the larva would suffocate when it first hatched. By laying the egg in the neck, she ensures that the newly hatched larva can get air as well as food. As it grows bigger and stronger, it eats its way deeper into the pear.

But what about the beetles who buried the ball?

Several hours later, the father pops out of the soil. He crouches beside the burrow and settles down for a nap. The next day the mother appears. The father shakes himself awake, and together they head back to the dung pile to carve out another ball. Père is delighted to find that the beetle husband remains faithful to his beetle wife. Père points out that in spite of living on sheep droppings, these little beetles have high moral standards!

The Sacred Beetle

The scarab is over an inch long and is the largest and most famous of our dung beetles. In the summer, we see them in the cow pastures rolling around huge balls of dung, many times bigger than themselves. After burying the balls, the beetles feast at their leisure in their underground dining rooms. The ancient Egyptians saw the ball as a symbol of the sun traveling across the sky, and so they named the scarab the sacred beetle. They thought that the ball contained the beetle's egg, but—like the Sisyphus—the female lays her egg in a pear-shaped home. The first time Père opened up a scarab's burrow and found a beetle putting the finishing touches to her pear, he says that he was as excited as if he'd been digging through relics in ancient Egypt and had uncovered a sacred insect carved in emerald.

The scarab wears a six-toothed curved rake on its head for collecting and sorting the dung. The bow-shaped front legs are strong-toothed tools with which it pushes the material back between its four hind legs. It uses its back legs to shape the ball against its belly. As the beetle adds more dung, the ball grows bigger—as big as a walnut, then as big as an apple, and sometimes even as big as a man's fist.

Sometimes a beetle takes a partner—though it's nearer the truth to say that the partner takes him. This second beetle is a lazy fellow who has flown in, hoping for a free meal. Although he pretends to help, he mostly perches on top of the ball, letting the first beetle do all the work. Even when the first beetle starts to dig the burrow, the other one doesn't help. He just sits on top of the ball, pretending to guard it. The first beetle grows uneasy. Every now and then, he pops out of the burrow to make sure that everything is all right. He nudges the ball closer to the hole so that he can keep an eye on it. But as the burrow gets deeper, it gets harder for him to keep checking. Now the thief sees his chance and makes off with the ball. The first beetle, sensing that all is not right, scrambles back to the surface and immediately takes off after his precious ball. When he catches up, the thief pretends that he was only trying to stop the ball from rolling away. The first beetle apparently believes him, even though the ground is flat. The two beetles roll the ball back together, complete the tunnel, and share the feast.

The story, however, doesn't always end on a friendly

note. Sometimes when the first beetle catches the thief, there's a fight. The winner gets the ball, and the loser flies off to look for a fresh patch of dung. Or he may look for another beetle with a ball and continue his thieving ways.

One afternoon, Père plays a trick on two scarabs. As usual, one of them is getting a free ride. Without disturbing the resting beetle, Père pushes a long, straight pin through the ball, nailing it to the earth. The beetle who is doing the pushing soon realizes that he has hit an obstacle. He walks around the ball two or three times, inspecting it. Nothing seems to be amiss. He goes back to work. The ball still doesn't move.

"Let's look up above," he seems to say. Climbing up, he finds nothing but his sleeping helper. You'd think he would rouse him and say, "What are you doing there, lazybones? Come and look at this thing; it's broken down!" But he ignores him and studies the ball again from ground level.

The sleeping beetle finally gets the message that things are not going the way they should. He scrambles down and begins to push, but two beetles prove to be no better than one. By now both of them are growing agitated. You can tell by the way little red fans on the end of their antennae open and shut and open again.

Then one of them seems to say, "What's underneath?"

After a little digging around, they discover the pin. Will they cut the ball apart and free it? No! Instead the two beetles slip under the ball, one on either side of the pin, and heave with their backs. The ball slides up the pin. Finally it is high enough to drop free.

Père wants to try the experiment again, this time with a longer pin. But he decides to look for another pair of beetles. These two have earned their dinner!

The Noisy Cicada

The peasants claim that at harvesttime the cicada hides in the bushes, shouting, "Sego! Sego! Sego! Reap! Reap! Reap!"

La Fontaine also thinks the cicada is a lazy fellow, who makes a lot of noise but expects others to do all the work. According to the fable, the cicada sings all summer, while the ant is busy storing provisions. When winter comes, the hungry cicada goes to the ant and begs for food.

"Why didn't you gather it in the summer when it was plentiful?" the ant asks him.

"I was too busy singing," the cicada replies.

"Then now you may dance," the ant says unkindly.

Père says that La Fontaine has the story backwards. In the trees by our front door, the ant is the beggar and the cicada is the provider. Hundreds of cicadas spend the summer in our plane trees, boring into the smooth bark and quenching their thirst on sap. Père points out the tiny ants that seem to be attacking the giant cicadas. One crawls under a cicada and nibbles at its legs. Another climbs onto the cicada's back and tugs on its wings. The big insect eventually loses patience. It pulls its sucking mouth out of the bark and moves away. The ants then nip in and drink from the sap spring, which soon dries up with no cicada to tend it.

Today, however, we are more interested in the noisy cicadas than in the thieving ants. The cicada is a drummer. Its instrument is built into its plump body. At the base of each hind wing is a patch of skin, or membrane, stretched over a cavity in the abdomen. When the insect vibrates the membrane, the sound echoes in the cavity.

Most people think that cicadas sing to attract a mate. But on our plane trees, the cicadas are already lined up in pairs. Père says that you don't spend months on end calling to someone who is at your elbow! Besides, he claims that cicadas are deaf. Although they have good eyesight and fall silent when something moves, when we stand behind them and make a noise, they keep right on singing. We've tried talking, whistling, and clapping our hands. Père is now about to carry out his greatest experiment. At least, Anna, Marie-Pauline, and I think so. Mother, on the other hand, is looking worried.

The only other person present for this big test of the ci-

cadas' reaction to noise is the gunner, who is loading the artillery.

Yes! Père went down to the village and borrowed the two cannons that are usually fired only to celebrate Patron Saint's Day.

"Are we ready?" Père asks. "Are all the windows open?"

Mother nods. The blast might break the glass if the windows were closed.

"Everyone listen!" Père orders.

We all tune our ears to the never-ending song of the cicada. We listen to the depth and rhythm of the song.

The gun goes off with a noise like thunder.

The cicadas keep right on singing. We all agree that the volume and rhythm have not changed.

The second gun is fired, with no more effect than the first. I'd like to do the experiment one more time, but Père says he has proved his point.

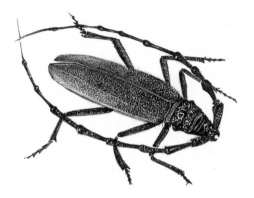

The Capricorn Beetle

The man we buy our firewood from smiles when Père asks for pulpy, worm-eaten trunks. Doesn't he know that sound wood burns hotter? He does, but when it comes time to split the trunks into logs, Père is satisfied with the bargain that he struck. The wood is riddled with winding tunnels carved out by the larvae of the capricorn beetle. The fat grubs will provide him with something to think about during the winter.

These grubs are truly strange creatures. Père describes them as bits of crawling intestine. The black armored head has chisel jaws designed for tunneling through hard wood. The rest of the animal's body is clothed in skin as fine as satin and as white as ivory. The legs are not properly developed and are no use for walking. The grub has pads on its back and stomach, which it can puff out and shrink at will. This enables it to move forward as it eats its way through the wood. Digested wood fills the tunnel behind it.

The capricorn spends three years inside an oak tree before turning into a handsome long-horned beetle. The grubs in Père's logs come in two sizes. The bigger ones are as thick as his finger; the smaller ones, which are in their first year, are about the size of my little finger. We also find motionless pupae, waiting for warm weather to signal that it's time to emerge as adults.

When we take a closer look at a grub, we discover that it has no eyes. It has no need for them inside the pitch-dark tunnels. It doesn't react when we scratch the wood close to it, imitating the sound of another grub tunneling, so we think it doesn't hear. Nor does it respond when we put strong-smelling camphor in its tunnel. It has no sense of smell. We can't tell if it tastes the wood that continually passes through its chomping jaws. That leaves only the sense of touch. We know that it can feel because it quivers when we poke it.

The capricorn grub is a half-alive, nothing-at-all sort of animal. It experiences its world with only one or maybe two senses. Yet this insect, which hardly knows the present, is able to foresee the future! The grub plans, well in advance, for the great moment when it will be a full-grown

beetle. One day it turns its back on the safety of the heart-
wood and tunnels toward the outside, where a woodpecker
may be waiting, hoping for a fat little sausage for dinner.
The grub gnaws almost all the way through the bark, leav-
ing only a thin screen. It seems to know that when it is
a grown beetle, it will no longer be able to cut through
wood.

The grub then retreats a short way down the tunnel. Its
next job is to carve out a little room about three or four
inches long, and little wider than it is high. It lines the
chamber with shredded wood fiber, as soft as swan's down.
It packs a layer of sawdust in the exit passage. It seals off the
passage with an acorn-shaped, chalky lid that it manufac-
tured in its stomach.

When the busy grub has finally finished its work, it lies
down on the soft mattress, sheds its skin, and becomes a
motionless pupa. But it always makes one careful last
preparation. It lies with its head pointing toward the exit.

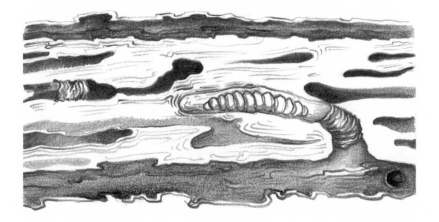

When warm weather comes, the beetle sheds its pupal skin. It now wears stiff horny armor, and has bright eyes and long, sensitive antennae. The way to freedom lies ahead. The beetle picks at the chalky lid with its claws and pushes it aside. When it breaks through the last screen, it sees the world for the first time, its antennae quivering with excitement.

Now when we find a pupa lying with its head pointing toward the outside, we have a new respect for that bit of crawling intestine it used to be. The grub knew that the adult beetle, encased in stiff armor and hampered by long antennae, would not be able to turn around in the little room. If the grub lay down facing the wrong way, the chamber would be the beetle's tomb.

"In capricorn beetles the stages of life are the opposite of ours," Père says. "They have it all backwards. For them youth is the season of stubborn work, energy, and strong tools. Adult age is the season of leisure and idleness."

Anna, Marie-Pauline, and I don't agree with Père. We are young. We may not have strong tools, but our days are filled with stubborn work and energy! Whereas for some of the adults we know, winter, at least, is a season of leisure. By four o'clock in the afternoon we can count on finding Favier sitting by the chimney corner in the kitchen, puffing on his pipe. Though he's not exactly idle. While Mother prepares the dinner, Favier entertains the whole household with stories of the battles he fought long ago and of the distant places he has seen. He tells us of strange meals he's eaten—sea urchins in Constantinople and starlings in the Crimea, badger's back and the eyed lizard browned in oil. We are all beginning to lose our appetite for Mother's stew simmering on the hearth!

The Great Peacock Evening

This afternoon we are celebrating! Père's new book has just arrived from the printer. Although it isn't quite dark outside, Père lights the lamp and closes the curtains to shut out the gray November rain. He opens the book somewhere near the middle and begins to read:

"It was a memorable evening. I shall call it the Great Peacock Evening. Who does not know the magnificent moth, the largest in Europe, clad in maroon velvet, with a necktie of white fur? The wings, with their sprinkling of gray and brown, are crossed by a faint zigzag and edged with smoky white. In their center is a round patch, a great eye with a black pupil and an iris containing black, white, chestnut, and purple arcs.

"On the morning of the sixth of May, a female moth

emerges from her cocoon on the table in my study. I cover her, still damp from hatching, with a wire-mesh cage. I have no particular plans. I cage her from mere habit because I'm always on the lookout for what might happen.

"At nine o'clock, just as the household is going to bed, there is a great stir in the room next to mine. Little Paul is rushing about, jumping and stamping, and knocking over chairs like a mad thing. I hear him call me:

" 'Come quick, Père!' he shouts. 'Come and see these moths as big as birds! The room is full of them!'

"I hurry in. There is enough to justify the child's enthusiastic exclamations. It is an invasion the like of which I have never seen, the raid of the giant moths! Four are already caught in the birdcage. Others, more numerous, are fluttering on the ceiling.

"At the sight of them, I recall the prisoner of the morning.

" 'Leave your cage, Paul, and come with me,' I say. 'We will see something interesting!' "

The pulpy log that burns bravely in the fireplace is not responsible for the warm glow I feel as Père continues to read about the Great Peacock Evening. People everywhere are going to hear about how we tried to solve the mystery of the forty suitors that came looking for the prisoner in the dark.

"Am I in the book, too?" little Anna wants to know when Père reaches the end of the chapter.

"Of course," Père answers. "After all, you children are my eyes and my ears."

Anna, Marie-Pauline,and I grin at one another. We have finally caught up with Emile, Jules, Lucie, and the others.

"Read some more," Anna begs.

Père flips through the pages. "Here's a chapter about another memorable evening!" he says. "The night that Marius and the schoolmaster came for dinner and we ate roasted cossus grubs!"

About Henri Fabre

Jean Henri Casimir Fabre was born on December 21, 1823, in Saint-Léons in southern France. All his life he was fascinated by insects. He can rightfully be called the father of experimental entomology. At a time when most other scientists were busy collecting and classifying, he was interested in behavior. He studied insects with great patience and inspiration.

Fabre kept to himself. He didn't interact with many other scientists or read their published work. He did, however, have some famous friends. He and Charles Darwin wrote letters to each other. Darwin referred to him as "the incomparable observer," but Fabre never read *The Origin of Species* all the way through. Another friend was John Stuart Mill, the English philosopher, who lived in Avignon for a while. The two men often went for walks together, and when Fabre lost his teaching job, Mill lent him money so that he could move to Orange.

Much of Fabre's work has stood the test of time—but not all of it. His equipment was crude, and some of his descriptions of insects are not detailed enough for us to know the species he was working with. Also, advances in science have unraveled mysteries that baffled Fabre. Some seventy years after the Great Peacock Evening, scientists in Germany isolated a sex attractant, or pheromone, in a female moth. The chemical is so potent that it attracts male moths over a distance of two or three miles.

It wasn't until 1910, when Fabre was eighty-six years old and had only five more years to live, that his genius was recognized. A jubilee celebration was held in Sérignan in his honor. The President of France came to visit. A statue was erected in the village. Fabre wanted only one word on the statue: *Laboremus*, which is Latin for "Let us work."

As well as being a great scientist, Fabre was a wonderful writer. Maybe it's fortunate that he didn't steep himself in other scientists' books. His writing style is very much his own, full of humor and unexpected comparisons. His ten volumes of *Souvenirs Entomologiques* make for good reading, although they are rather wordy by today's standards. In *Children of Summer,* to give the flavor of Fabre's writing, I let Paul speak with many of his father's vivid words and phrases—though, of course, Fabre wrote and spoke in

French. Most of the episodes were selected because Paul was specifically mentioned as a helper. Fabre obviously enjoyed sharing his studies with his children as much as they enjoyed being part of the great adventure.

Glossary

abdomen: The third part of an insect's body. The other two parts are the head and the thorax.

antenna (plural, antennae): Feelers on the head of an insect.

arachnid: One of the classes of animals. Arachnids are invertebrates and have eight legs and bodies with two parts.

cocoon: The envelope that protects the pupa.

entomologist: A scientist who studies insects.

harmas: Land that is not good for agriculture. Fabre's home in Sérignan, which is now a museum, is still known as "The Harmas," though the gardens are dense with flowers and trees.

insect: One of the classes of animals. Insects are invertebrates (they have no internal skeleton). Adult insects have six legs and bodies with three parts—head, thorax, and abdomen.

larva (plural, larvae): The stage of an insect between the egg and the pupa. Caterpillars and grubs are other names for larvae. "Caterpillar" is used for the larva of a moth or a butterfly. "Grub" is often used for a beetle larva.

mandible: An insect's jaw.

ovipositor: An egg-laying tool at the end of the abdomen.

Père: The French word for father.

pupa (plural, pupae): The resting stage when the insect larva changes to an adult.

saxicola: Belongs to a group of birds that includes the wheatear and stonechat.

social insects: Insects, such as the honeybee, that live together in a community.

thorax: The section of the insect's body to which the wings and legs are attached.

Index